DO THE WORK!
PEACE, JUSTICE, AND STRONG INSTITUTIONS MEETS PARTNERSHIPS FOR THE GOALS

COMMITTING TO THE UN'S SUSTAINABLE DEVELOPMENT GOALS

JULIE KNUTSON

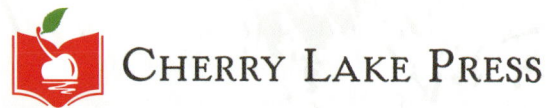

Published in the United States of America by Cherry Lake Publishing Group
Ann Arbor, Michigan
www.cherrylakepublishing.com

Reading Adviser: Beth Walker Gambro, MS, Ed., Reading Consultant, Yorkville, IL

Photo Credits: © trabantos/Shutterstock.com, cover, 1; © Everett Collection/Shutterstock.com, 5; Infographic From The Sustainable Development Goals Report 2021, by United Nations Department of Economic and Social Affairs © 2021 United Nations. Reprinted with the permission of the United Nations, 7, 8; © Michal Urbanek/Shutterstock.com, 9; © MintArt/Shutterstock.com, 10; © Vic Hinterlang/Shutterstock.com, 13; © NataliAlba/Shutterstock.com, 14; © vesperstock/Shutterstock.com, 17; © Anna Pasichnyk/Shutterstock.com, 18; © Monkey Business Images/Shutterstock.com, 19, 21; © wavebreakmedia/Shutterstock.com, 22; © DGLimages/Shutterstock.com, 23; © Rido/Shutterstock.com, 24; © Diego G Diaz/Shutterstock.com, 27

Copyright © 2023 by Cherry Lake Publishing Group
All rights reserved. No part of this book may be reproduced or utilized in any form or by any means without written permission from the publisher.

Cherry Lake Press is an imprint of Cherry Lake Publishing Group.

Library of Congress Cataloging-in-Publication Data
Names: Knutson, Julie, author.
Title: Do the work! : peace, justice, and strong institutions meets partnerships for the goals / by Julie Knutson.
Description: Ann Arbor, Michigan : Cherry Lake Publishing, [2022] | Series: Committing to the UN's sustainable development goals | Includes bibliographical references. | Audience: Grades 4-6
Identifiers: LCCN 2022005356 | ISBN 9781668909287 (hardcover) | ISBN 9781668910887 (paperback) | ISBN 9781668914069 (pdf) | ISBN 9781668912478 (ebook)
Subjects: LCSH: Social justice—Juvenile literature. | Toleration—Juvenile literature. | Equality—Juvenile literature. | Sustainable development—Juvenile literature.
Classification: LCC HM671 .K658 2022 | DDC 303.3/72—dc23/eng/20220210
LC record available at https://lccn.loc.gov/2022005356

Cherry Lake Publishing Group would like to acknowledge the work of the Partnership for 21st Century Learning, a Network of Battelle for Kids. Please visit http://www.battelleforkids.org/networks/p21 for more information.

Printed in the United States of America
Corporate Graphics

The content of this publication has not been approved by the United Nations and does not reflect the views of the United Nations or its officials or Member States. For more information on the Sustainable Development Goals, please visit https://www.un.org/sustainabledevelopment.

ABOUT THE AUTHOR

Julie Knutson is an author-educator who writes extensively about global citizenship and the Sustainable Development Goals. Her previous book, *Global Citizenship: Engage in the Politics of a Changing World* (Nomad Press, 2020), introduces key concepts about 21st-century interconnectedness to middle grade and high school readers. She hopes that this series will inspire young readers to take action and embrace their roles as changemakers in the world.

TABLE OF CONTENTS

CHAPTER 1
Meet the SDGs **4**

CHAPTER 2
Why Do We Have Goals? **12**

CHAPTER 3
Do the Work! Contribute to the Goals at Home **16**

CHAPTER 4
Do the Work! Contribute to the Goals at School ... **20**

CHAPTER 5
**Do the Work! Contribute to the Goals
in Your Community** **26**

EXTEND YOUR LEARNING 29
FURTHER RESEARCH 30
GLOSSARY 31
INDEX 32

CHAPTER 1

Meet the SDGs

In the late 1940s, people across the planet were scarred by the experience of World War II (1939–1945). The total number of people who died in this war, including in the **Holocaust**, is anywhere from 35 million to 60 million. Two out of three European Jewish people were murdered during the war. In Eastern Europe, the country of Poland lost 20 percent of its population. And in Japan, Hiroshima and Nagasaki lost an estimated 140,000 and 74,000 people, respectively, when U.S. forces dropped **atomic bombs** on the cities.

How could the world recover from a disaster this huge? How could people ensure that war and destruction on this scale never happened again?

Fighting in World War II wasn't limited to battlefields. According to *Britannica*, "In Great Britain about 30 percent of the homes were destroyed or damaged; in France, Belgium, and the Netherlands about 20 percent" of homes suffered the same fate.

What Are the SDGs?

Today, the **United Nations** (UN) continues to work toward building peace and forging partnerships between countries. In 2015, it reaffirmed its commitment to creating a better world "For People and the Planet" through the **Sustainable** Development Goals (SDGs). All 193 UN member states have agreed to cooperate in reaching the 169 SDG targets by 2030. The goals range from "No Poverty" (SDG 1) to "Quality Education" (SDG 4) to "Climate Action" (SDG 13). The final two SDGs, "Peace, Justice, and Strong Institutions" (SDG 16) and "Partnership for the Goals" (SDG 17), push for the full realization of the UN's mission.

Related Goals

By their nature, the SDGs operate as a system. Action in one area will have a positive impact on another. How do SDGs 16 and 17 relate to the others on the list? Consider these examples:

Ensuring "Peace, Justice, and Strong Institutions" means guaranteeing that all people have equal rights, regardless of race, gender, sexual orientation, age, class, or ability status. For **inequalities** between people and groups to truly be reduced—the aim of SDG 10—inequalities in our laws and justice systems also have to be eliminated.

16 PEACE, JUSTICE AND STRONG INSTITUTIONS

PROMOTE PEACEFUL AND INCLUSIVE SOCIETIES FOR SUSTAINABLE DEVELOPMENT, PROVIDE ACCESS TO JUSTICE FOR ALL AND BUILD EFFECTIVE, ACCOUNTABLE AND INCLUSIVE INSTITUTIONS AT ALL LEVELS

THE PANDEMIC IS INTENSIFYING CHILDREN'S RISK OF EXPLOITATION
INCLUDING

TRAFFICKING AND CHILD LABOUR

1 IN 3 TRAFFICKING VICTIMS WERE CHILDREN (2018)

CHILD LABOUR ROSE TO **160 MILLION** (2020)

FIRST INCREASE IN TWO DECADES

IN 2020, THE KILLINGS OF **331 HUMAN RIGHTS DEFENDERS** WERE REPORTED IN **32 COUNTRIES**

AN **18% INCREASE** FROM 2019

ONLY 82 COUNTRIES HAD **INDEPENDENT NATIONAL HUMAN RIGHTS INSTITUTIONS** IN COMPLIANCE WITH INTERNATIONAL STANDARDS (2020)

BRIBERY IS AT LEAST FIVE TIMES MORE LIKELY IN

LOW-INCOME COUNTRIES **37.6%** — THAN IN — HIGH-INCOME COUNTRIES **7.2%**

THE SUSTAINABLE DEVELOPMENT GOALS REPORT 2021: UNSTATS.UN.ORG/SDGS/REPORT/2021/

17 PARTNERSHIPS FOR THE GOALS

STRENGTHEN THE MEANS OF IMPLEMENTATION AND REVITALIZE THE GLOBAL PARTNERSHIP FOR SUSTAINABLE DEVELOPMENT

NET ODA REACHED A RECORD HIGH OF **$161 BILLION** IN 2020

REPRESENTING **0.32%** OF DONORS' GNI

BUT STILL SHORT OF THE TARGET OF **0.7%** OF GNI

DEFYING PREDICTIONS, REMITTANCE FLOWS TO LOW- AND MIDDLE-INCOME COUNTRIES REACHED **$540 BILLION** IN 2020

ONLY **1.6% BELOW** 2019 LEVEL

FOREIGN DIRECT INVESTMENT DROPPED BY UP TO **40%**

$1.5 TRILLION (2019)

BELOW $1 TRILLION (2020)

NEARLY HALF OF THE GLOBAL POPULATION — 3.7 BILLION PEOPLE — ARE STILL NOT ONLINE

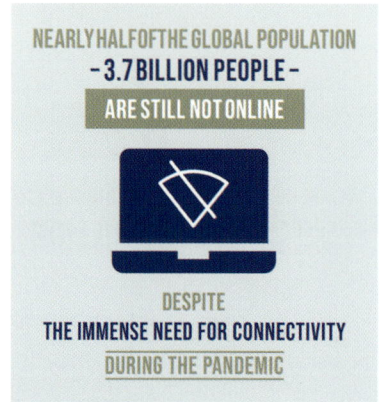

DESPITE THE IMMENSE NEED FOR CONNECTIVITY DURING THE PANDEMIC

63% OF LOW-INCOME AND LOWER-MIDDLE-INCOME COUNTRIES ARE IN NEED OF **ADDITIONAL FINANCING FOR DATA AND STATISTICS** TO FACE THE CHALLENGES POSED BY THE PANDEMIC

THE SUSTAINABLE DEVELOPMENT GOALS REPORT 2021: UNSTATS.UN.ORG/SDGS/REPORT/2021/

The killing of people including George Floyd, Breonna Taylor, and Daunte Wright focused attention on the sometimes fatally different treatment of African Americans by the police. These inequalities resulted in national and international protests during and beyond 2020.

Do you want to see action on **climate change** (SDG 13)? Or improved education for all children (SDG 4)? Progress requires partnership. No one individual, group, or country can have the full responsibility of making gains on the SDGs. People have to work together across organizations, nations, and boundaries. We need to work in "Partnership for the Goals." So let's get started!

The SDGs are an extension of the UN's mission.

How Do You Define "Peace"?

The United Nations, an international organization to promote peace and cooperation between countries, was established after World War II. Its founding **charter**, written in 1945, explained its purpose:

THE PEOPLES OF THE UNITED NATIONS DETERMINED

*To save succeeding generations from the **scourge** of war, which twice in our lifetime has brought untold sorrow to mankind, and*

*to reaffirm faith in fundamental **human rights**, in the dignity and worth of the human person, in the equal rights of men and women and of nations large and small, and*

*to establish conditions under which justice and respect for the obligations arising from **treaties** and other sources of international law can be maintained, and*

to promote social progress and better standards of life in larger freedom,

AND FOR THESE ENDS

To practice tolerance and live together in peace with one another as good neighbors, and

to unite our strength to maintain international peace and security, and

to ensure, by the acceptance of principles and the institution of methods, that armed force shall not be used, save in the common interest, and

to employ international machinery for the promotion of the economic and social advancement of all peoples.

CHAPTER 2

Why Do We Have Goals?

So you want to ace math this year, finishing with an A+ on your report card. Or you want to get a speaking role in the school play or make the basketball team. These are all examples of goals. To reach a goal, you have to consciously work to achieve it. People who do that most successfully don't do it without a plan. They take steps to get from where they are now to where they want to be.

> **STOP AND THINK:** *Good goal-setting is sometimes guided by the "SMART" strategy, meaning that the goal is Specific, Measurable, Achievable, Relevant, and Timed. What goals do you have? Write them down and think about how you can make your goals "SMART."*

Violence and war uproot individuals and families all over the world. According to the UN, in 2019, "the number of people fleeing war, persecution, and conflict exceeded 79.5 million, the highest level ever recorded."

Freedom of information laws exist in 127 countries. This means that people have the right to access government documents and that governments cannot operate in secret.

The SDGs are a set of goals that can't be reached by one person or small group. Making progress on them requires the participation of *all* of us. But what guidance is there for acting on them? Did the designers of the SDGs make them SMART goals to which all people could contribute? The short answer is yes.

Each of the 17 SDGs has targets and **indicators**. These targets and indicators monitor progress on the goals. They also help people see what further measures are needed.

For success on SDGs 16 and 17, the UN member states need to meet a series of targets by 2030. These targets include things like reducing violence and investing in technology.

CHAPTER 3

Do the Work! Contribute to the Goals at Home

Creating peace, justice, and partnerships for the greater good begins at home. The way we interact with and treat our siblings, parents, grandparents, and caregivers is a reflection of our place in the broader world. Here are some examples of everyday actions you can take to make a difference on SDGs 16 and 17.

- **Learn and Educate** — Read about the causes of war and conflict. Learn about inequalities in your community. Research the forces and factors that lead **refugees** to seek **asylum** in other countries. Talk with family members about what you learn. What can you do as a family to address these challenges? Whether volunteering, joining protests, or writing to your elected officials, no action is too small.

Participating in elections is an important part of the democratic process. Talk with your parents about voting. What does this right mean to them?

- **Be Mindful** — How do you want to relate to others? How do you want the people you live with to think about your behavior? Take a few minutes at the end of each day to think about these questions. Were you your best self today? What can you change for tomorrow? Building good relationships at home will follow you into school and your community.

[DO THE WORK! PEACE, JUSTICE, AND STRONG INSTITUTIONS MEETS PARTNERSHIPS FOR THE GOALS]

Practice teamwork at home! Whether helping with yard work or playing a board game, you can work on building your skills with others in your household.

In your house, do some people think they do more chores or tasks than others? Discuss this as a family.

- **Talk About It!** — Does everyone in your household feel like they are treated fairly and equally? Do you ever lose your temper with your parents, siblings, or neighbors? Talk about what you're feeling and come up with ways as a group to create a better place for everyone to live.

  STOP AND THINK: *When pondering big topics like the causes of war or the sources of inequality, you can begin by asking "why?" This process of questioning will allow you to get closer to the roots of the issue.*

CHAPTER 4

Do the Work! Contribute to the Goals at School

For many of us, schools are places where we learn not only facts and numbers but also how to manage conflict, compromise, and work cooperatively with others. Schools offer many opportunities to put SDGs 16 and 17 into practice.

- **Play** — What do theater, soccer, basketball, and band have in common? They're all activities that require people to work together! They provide what people call "life skills," including managing conflict, developing strategies, and coming to agreements. Participating in school clubs and groups will help you now and in the future, giving you problem-solving and people skills needed to face both large and small challenges.

Authors of a 2019 study from the Cleveland Clinic noted that, "Through team sports, kids learn how to lead and negotiate with other kids to reach a common goal." The study also found that playing team sports can improve mental health.

- **Stand Up Against Bullying** — Bullying, whether physical or verbal, is a form of violence. Make your school a place where bullying is not acceptable. StopBullying.gov, a project of the U.S. Department of Health and Human Services, recommends taking these actions:
  — *Treat Everyone with Respect:* Don't say or do hurtful things, and remember that all people are different and deserve respect. If you've been mean or rude to someone in the past, apologize, and do better in the future.

Treat others the way you want to be treated!

- *Protect Yourself from Cyberbullying:* Think about what you post and where, and keep your passwords private. Talk to a trusted adult about any confusing or hurtful messages that you see online.
- *Stand Up for Others:* If you witness bullying, report it to an adult. Be kind to the student who is being bullied. Think about how you would want to be treated in the same situation and live that way.

During the COVID-19 pandemic, cyberbullying increased as students spent more time online.

Talk with teachers about inviting community members to your school to share their expertise.

— *Get Involved:* Create posters about the harmful effects of bullying and ask permission to post them at school. Talk with teachers and your principal about how your school can prevent bullying from happening. You can partner with classmates and adults to make a difference!

- **Encourage Partnerships** — Bringing local leaders into the classroom allows you to learn more about organizations working for social change. These individuals can also tell you more about what you can do to help make the SDGs a reality.
- **Host a Fundraiser or Food Drive** — You and your classmates can partner with **nonprofit** organizations by hosting a fundraiser or food drive. Through events like garage sales or walk-a-thons, you can contribute money and resources to fund their operations.

Restorative Justice

Just what is "restorative justice"? Think about it as an "open collaborative circle where students can talk about their feelings on topics of their choice," explains educator Rachel Saathoff. Saathoff teaches children of a variety of ages how to resolve problems in peaceful ways. She offers these tips for creating peaceful classrooms and constructively addressing conflict:
1. Walk away and use a coping skill—for example, deep breathing, squeezing a stress ball, or listening to music.
2. If you are having a conflict with someone, tell them how you feel.
3. Talk to an adult you trust.

CHAPTER 5

Do the Work! Contribute to the Goals in Your Community

In many parts of the world, the UN Charter goal to "reaffirm faith in fundamental human rights, in the dignity and worth of the human person, in the equal rights of men and women and of nations large and small" has yet to be met. Take action in your community to help realize this target.

- **Learn and Educate** — Does the justice system in your community treat all people equally? Are there laws that discriminate against people based on their identity? Does your city, state, or national government make it easy for all people to participate in elections? These are some of the questions you can ask to determine how well your community is doing at meeting SDG 16.

Work to ensure that all people are seen, respected, and have a voice.

- **Speak Out** — Once you have answers to the questions above, learn about what organizations are working to address these issues. Partner with them. Write letters to your elected officials **advocating** for peace, justice, and equality.

Kid Actors Collaborating Across Continents

In spring 2021, six young actors from India and six from the United States teamed up to form a virtual theater company. The focus? The SDGs! The "Global Artists for Sustainability" project was sponsored by Pomegranate Workshop in Mumbai, India, and Chicago Children's Theatre. The project **exemplifies** SDG 17, "Partnership for the Goals."

Over six Saturdays, the group of 9- to 12-year-olds met online. They wrote a script and recorded a film on Zoom. The film features a group of fearless school kids from the future who travel back in time to learn about life in 2021. The future-kids marvel at things now extinct and at the odd habits of their not-so-distant ancestors.

As the time travelers talk about their journey, one young actor exclaims, "I have an idea! Let's leave behind a message for the people of 2021, like a little reverse time capsule." That message, told in turn by each cast member, is as follows:

> "You have to work faster—and harder—to save the environment. And you cannot do that without women and men and **non-binary** people being treated equally."

This message addresses the twin aspects of the SDGs—improving life for all people and the planet. Let's take their advice for the sake of our present and future!

Extend Your Learning

Make an SDGs Coloring Book

Now that you know about the SDGs, teach others about them! Make a coloring book for younger students that explains what the SDGs are and what they aim to achieve. Here are some ideas for getting started:

- Include a coloring page for each goal, complete with a colorable symbol that represents it. For example, a page for "Quality Education" (SDG 4) could have a school building.
- Clearly state what the SDG is and note some of its targets.
- Offer actions that people can take at home, school, or in the community to help make progress on this goal.

Share this resource with family members, younger children at your school, and your local librarian to launch your own partnerships for the SDGs!

Further Research

BOOKS

Harasymiw, Therese. *You Can Help Stop Bullying!* New York, NY: PowerKids Press, 2021.

Tyner, Artika R. *Black Lives Matter: From Hashtag to the Streets.* Minneapolis, MN: Lerner Publications, 2021.

Winn, Kevin, and Kelisa Wing. *Voting Rights.* Ann Arbor, MI: Cherry Lake Publishing, 2021.

WEBSITES

Goal 16: Promote Just, Peaceful and Inclusive Societies—United Nations Sustainable Development
https://www.un.org/sustainabledevelopment/peace-justice
Check out the UN's Sustainable Development Goals website for more information on Goal 16.

Goal 17: Revitalize the Global Partnership for Sustainable Development—United Nations Sustainable Development
https://www.un.org/sustainabledevelopment/globalpartnerships
Check out the UN's Sustainable Development Goals website for more information on Goal 17.

The Global Goals of Sustainable Development
https://www.margreetdeheer.com/the-global-goals-of-sustainable-development
Check out these free comics about the United Nations Sustainable Development Goals.

Glossary

advocating (AD-vuh-kay-ting) supporting or arguing on behalf of something

asylum (uh-SYE-luhm) a safe and protected place

atomic bombs (uh-TAH-mik BAHMZ) nuclear weapons

charter (CHAHR-tuhr) a founding document

climate change (KLY-muht CHANJ) significant changes in Earth's climate and weather, due to factors such as global warming

exemplifies (ig-ZEM-pluh-fyz) serves as an example of

Holocaust (HOH-luh-kost) the mass slaughter of European civilians, especially Europe's Jewish population, by the Nazis during World War II

human rights (HYOO-muhn RITES) rights that belong to all people on the planet, enshrined in the UN's universal declaration of human rights

indicators (in-duh-KAY-tuhrs) measurements of progress

inequalities (ih-nih-KWAH-luh-teez) when some people have more rights or opportunities than others

non-binary (nahn-BYE-nuh-ree) a person who does not identify as either entirely male or female

nonprofit (nahn-PRAH-fuht) an organization that does not seek to make a profit

refugees (reh-fyoo-JEEZ) people who flee one country to another to escape persecution

scourge (SKURJ) a harsh punishment

sustainable (suh-STAY-nuh-buhl) able to be maintained at a certain rate

treaties (TREE-teez) agreements between countries

United Nations (yuh-NYE-tuhd NAY-shuhns) the international organization that promotes peace and cooperation among nations

INDEX

acting, 28
activism. *See* personal actions
art, 28–29

Black Lives Matter movement, 9
bribery, 7
bullying, 21–24

charitable giving, 25
child labor, 7
children's theatre, 28
chores, 18–19
coloring books, 29
community-based support of SDGs, 16, 25–28
conflict management, 20–22, 25
COVID-19 pandemic, 7, 23
cyberbullying, 22–23

discrimination, 26, 28
donations, 25

education, 16, 20, 26
elections, 17, 26

financial lending, 8
foreign investment, 8
freedom of information, 14
fundraisers, 25

goal-setting, 12, 15

Holocaust, 4
home-based support of SDGs, 16–19, 29
human rights institutions and goals, 6–7, 11, 26
human trafficking, 7

institutions, support of, 6–7
international law, 11
internet access, 8
interpersonal relationships, 17, 19–22

life skills, 20–22

mindfulness, 17

peace
  defining, 11
  personal actions for, 16–17, 21–22, 25
  SDGs goals/targets, 6–7
personal actions
  community-based support, 16, 25–28
  home-based support, 16–19, 29
  school-based support, 20–25, 29
personal relationships, 17–22
play, 20–21
police brutality, 9
political participation, 17, 26–27

racial inequality, 9
refugees, 13, 16
remittances, 8
restorative justice, 25

Saathoff, Rachel, 25
school-based support of SDGs, 20–25, 29
SMART goals, 12, 15
sports, 20, 21
sustainable development, 6, 8
Sustainable Development Goals (SDGs), 6–10, 15

teachers, 24
team sports, 20–21
theatre, 28

United Nations, 10–11
United Nations Sustainable Development Goals (SDGs), 6–10, 15

volunteering, 16
voting, 17, 26

war, 4–5, 11, 13
World War II, 4–5